Balancing Act

Ellen Stoll Walsh

Beach Lane Books

New York   London   Toronto   Sydney

BEACH LANE BOOKS
An imprint of Simon & Schuster Children's Publishing Division
1230 Avenue of the Americas, New York, New York 10020
Copyright © 2010 by Ellen Stoll Walsh
All rights reserved, including the right of reproduction in whole or in part in any form.
BEACH LANE BOOKS is a trademark of Simon & Schuster, Inc.
For information about special discounts for bulk purchases, please contact
Simon & Schuster Special Sales at 1-866-506-1949 or business@simonandschuster.com.
The Simon & Schuster Speakers Bureau can bring authors to your live event.
For more information or to book an event, contact the Simon & Schuster Speakers
Bureau at 1-866-248-3049 or visit our website at www.simonspeakers.com.
The text for this book is set in Bookman Old Style.
The illustrations for this book are rendered in cut paper.
Manufactured in the United States of America
1210 PCR

10 9 8 7 6 5
Library of Congress Cataloging-in-Publication Data
Walsh, Ellen Stoll.
Balancing act / Ellen Stoll Walsh.—1st ed.
p. cm.
Summary: Two mice have fun playing on a teeter-totter, but as more and larger friends
join them, it becomes increasingly difficult to stay balanced.
ISBN 978-1-4424-0757-2 (hardcover)
[1. Equilibrium—Fiction. 2. Seesaw—Fiction. 3. Animals—Fiction.] I. Title.
PZ7.W1675Bal 2010
[E]—dc22
2009047659

For John and Grace

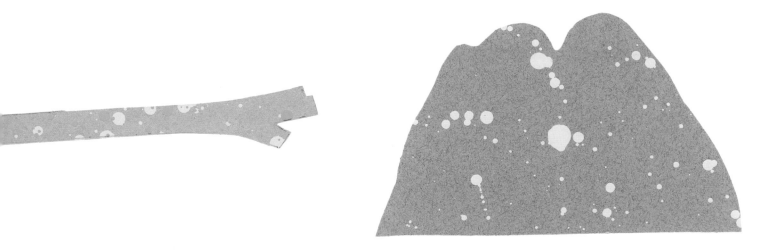

The mice made a teeter-totter.

It was fun to balance . . .

one mouse on each end.

Ta-da!

But then a salamander
wanted a turn.

Hmmm . . .

Luckily, a friend stepped in to help.

Perfect.
Balance again.

Uh-oh! A frog.

Whoa!

But then, another frog . . .

Ah, balance once more.

Oh, no! A bird wants to balance.

Whoops! *That's* not going to work!

Or maybe it will.

Ta-da!

But not for long.

Too many balancers.

Time for everyone to find something *else* to do.

Except the mice.

Ta-da!